For my little Else.
A kiss from your giant ~ C.N.

First published 2004 by Macmillan Children's Books
This edition published 2008 by Macmillan Children's Books
a division of Macmillan Publishers Limited
20 New Wharf Road, London N1 9RR
Basingstoke and Oxford
Associated companies throughout the world
www.panmacmillan.com

ISBN: 978-0-230-01816-7

Text copyright © Carl Norac 2004
Illustrations copyright © Ingrid Godon 2004
Moral rights asserted.

10 9 8 7 6 5 4 3 2 1

A CIP catalogue record for this book
is available from the British Library.

Printed in Malaysia by Tien Wah Press

CARL NORAC

My Daddy is a GIANT

Illustrated by Ingrid Godon

MACMILLAN CHILDREN'S BOOKS

My daddy is a giant.
When I want to cuddle him,
I have to climb a ladder.

When we play hide-and-seek,
my daddy has to hide
behind a mountain.

And when the clouds are tired, they come and sleep on my daddy's shoulders.

When my daddy sneezes,
it's like a hurricane.
It blows the sea away.

When my daddy laughs,

it's like another hurricane.

All the leaves fly off the trees.

Birds love my daddy.

They make their nests
in his hair.

When we play football,
my daddy always wins.

He can kick the ball as high as the moon.

But I always beat him at marbles.

His fingers are
far too big.

I like it when my daddy says,

"You're getting as tall as me!"

When my daddy runs,

the ground shakes

as if it was scared.

But I'm not scared
of anything when
I'm in my daddy's arms.

My daddy is a giant,
and he loves me with
all his giant heart.

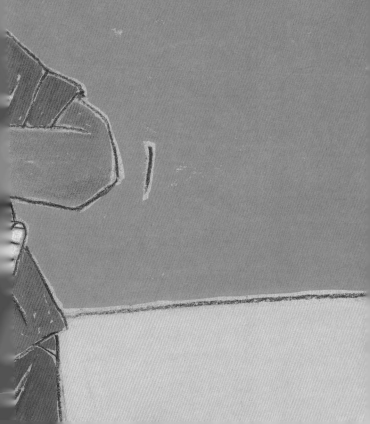